W9-AJR-443

The Band

Dina Anastasio

SCHOLASTIC INC.
New York Toronto London Auckland Sydney
Mexico City New Delhi Hong Kong Buenos Aires

For Isabella

Illustrations by Shingo Shimizu

The text in this edition has been revised from the original edition.

No part of this publication may be reproduced in whole or in part, or stored in a retrieval system, or transmitted in any form or by any means, electronic, mechanical, photocopying, recording, or otherwise, without written permission of the publisher. For information regarding permission, write to Scholastic Inc., 557 Broadway, New York, NY 10012.

Copyright © 2004, 1999 by Scholastic Inc.
Illustrations copyright © 2005 by Shingo Shimizu.
All rights reserved. Published by Scholastic Inc.
Printed in the U.S.A.

ISBN 0-439-66705-4

SCHOLASTIC, READ 180, and associated logos and designs are trademarks and/or registered trademarks of Scholastic Inc.

LEXILE is a registered trademark of MetaMetrics, Inc.

1 2 3 4 5 6 7 8 9 10   23   13 12 11 10 09 08 07 06 05

Contents

Max and Jake have big dreams for their band. All they need is their big break.

1 High Hopes

My name is Max. Music is my life. I've been playing the guitar for six years. People say I'm pretty good.

Last summer, I started a band with my best friend, Jake. Jake's a great drummer. Jake and I have been playing music together for a long time.

Tico and Matt joined our band awhile ago. Tico plays bass. Matt plays keyboard.

Jake was the glue that kept us together. His **timing** was perfect. When we were off, Jake slid us in again. When we missed, Jake brought us back.

Our band was called Octopus. Jake

chose the name because he said we should be reaching in all **directions**. He meant that we should **experiment**. That's Jake for you.

We played a lot of **local gigs**. Mostly, we played schools and parties. But we had bigger dreams than that. We wanted to play big shows. We wanted to be on MTV. In a few years, maybe we'd have a number-one hit.

Watch out world! Octopus was on the move.

Then, one night, it looked like one of our dreams really might come true.

Dee Brown called me.

"So, Max," she said. "When's the next gig?"

"Saturday night," I told her. "We're playing the high school dance. Why?"

"My dad wanted to know."

I knew all about Dee's dad. Everyone knew about Dee's dad. Dee Brown's father works for a big record company. Dee Brown's father is what we're all looking for. He's the real thing.

"Can you get him to the dance?" I asked.

"He'll be there," she said.

I told the rest of the band the next day.

"Yeah, sure," they said. They didn't believe me at first.

But then we got to work. We only had three days to get ready for Dee's father.

We practiced until midnight on Thursday. On Friday, we stopped early because we were all tired. But we were back at it at seven on Saturday morning.

Tico and Matt couldn't stop talking about what would happen when we got a record **deal**. We'd be rich. We'd be famous. People would want our autographs.

I was afraid to think about those things. I didn't know if we were good enough yet. Jake didn't say anything either. He seemed lost in his own thoughts.

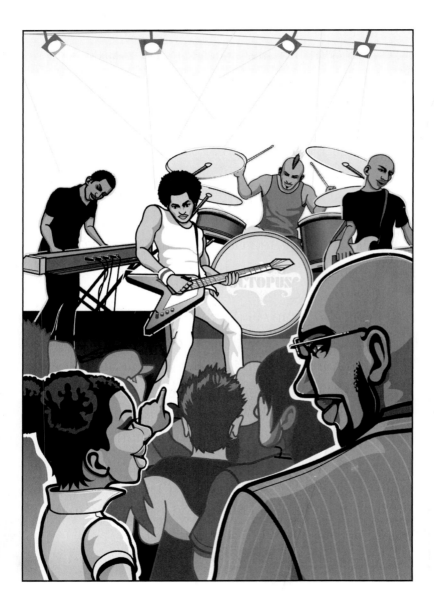

Saturday night was a great night. We played perfectly. The crowd loved us. That didn't matter, though. Only one person mattered. Dee Brown's father was there. He stood in the back corner with Dee the whole night. I didn't see him say one word. Not one.

This was our most important gig so far, and we played great. We were together. Jake led, and we followed. We were good. No one had to tell us that. We knew when we were good.

Dee's father walked over at the end of the gig.

"You're all right," he said. "What are you doing two weeks from Friday?"

Tico kept track of our gigs. "We don't have anything," he said.

"I'd like you to open for the J.C. Underground. They'll be playing in town. It's a last-minute thing."

"Sure," we all said. "Sure."

Who wouldn't want to open for the J.C.

Underground? They were really popular. The crowd would be huge.

"My boss will be there," Mr. Brown said. "He's the guy who makes the decisions."

We had two weeks to get ready.

What kind of pressure is the band under now?

Jake is busy with basketball practice. The band might be in trouble.

2 Trouble Begins

We started getting ready the next day.

Tico, Matt, and I were in my garage at five o'clock. Jake was an hour late.

"Sorry," he said. "Basketball started today."

I felt sick. I had forgotten about basketball. I had just been thinking about the band.

Music is my life. But it's not Jake's life. Music is just one thing in his life. Basketball is his real love.

That was the beginning of the end. When basketball started, the glue that held our band together began to come apart.

Jake was off that day. He lost the beat again and again. The timing wasn't there. I knew where it was. It was back in the gym. Jake's mind was on basketball.

The next day Jake showed up late again. His timing was worse than it had been the day before.

I could tell that Tico and Matt were mad. They tried to be nice. But I could tell.

"Let's play it again," Tico said.

We took it from the top. But we were still off. Jake wasn't with us.

Jake left early. He wanted to go home and practice basketball. The rest of us hung around the garage.

No one said anything. Then Tico said what we were all thinking.

"There's no way we're going to get a record deal," he said.

"Not a chance," Matt said.

"Anyone have any thoughts?" Tico asked.

He was looking at me. I had lots of thoughts. But I wasn't about to share them with anyone. I just shook my head.

I guess I knew what was coming.

"Maybe we should ask him to choose," Tico said. "Basketball or the band. What do you think, Max?"

I had to say something. So I said what was on my mind.

"Jake and I started this band together," I said. "It was his idea. He named it. He won't quit. And he won't give up basketball either. So, no. We can't ask him to choose."

"Are you sure he wants to be in this band?" Matt asked. "Are you really sure?"

"Of course I'm sure!" I said. I was beginning to get mad. Jake loved this band. He would not want to quit.

"Maybe you should find out," Tico suggested.

"I don't have to find out," I told them. "Jake wants to stay in the band. I don't want

to be in a band without him!"

That made them mad. They started to leave. I almost said I was sorry. But I didn't. I didn't because what I had said was true. Jake and I were a team. I couldn't play without him. Or could I?

"I'll talk to him," I said.

They didn't hear me. They were gone.

Do you think Max was right to stick up for Jake?

Maybe Jake really does have to choose between the band and basketball.

The Choice

I went over to Jake's place the next night. His mother said he was in the park. So that's where I went. He was shooting hoops.

I stood in the shadows and watched him. He was great. He couldn't miss—jump shots, three pointers, foul shots. It didn't matter. He was perfect.

He took a second to catch his breath. I called his name. He seemed glad to see me. We shot baskets for a while. Then we sat by the fence.

"How come we don't hang out anymore?" he asked.

"Everybody's busy, I guess."

We didn't say anything for a few minutes. I didn't know how to start. Then I did.

"Jake, maybe we should talk about the band," I said.

Jake watched me and waited.

"Tico thinks we should talk about the band," I said.

He frowned.

"The timing's been off a little lately," I said. "Tico and Matt are worried about it."

"Are you worried?" he asked.

"A little, I guess."

"Drumsticks are the mirror of the mind," he said.

I didn't get it.

"My mind is somewhere else," he said. "My mind is somewhere around the foul line."

Then I said it. I just came right out with it. "They think you should choose," I said.

I didn't want to hear his answer. I didn't want to know if he was mad. I didn't want to know if he wasn't. He was my friend. I didn't want him to leave the band *or* quit basketball.

I stood up and started to walk away. Jake stopped me. Somehow he knew what was on my mind.

"You're a good guitar player," he said. "You don't need me."

He was wrong. I did need him. I wasn't a good guitar player without him.

As I walked away, I heard him bouncing the ball. Tap, tap, tap. His timing was perfect.

Do you think Jake will choose the band or basketball?

It's the big night. And the band has to play without its favorite drummer.

4 Keeping Time

I couldn't sleep that night. I kept thinking about what Jake had said. Could I really play without him? Or would my playing be linked to Jake's forever? I knew what the answer should be. But I didn't like it.

Jake told me later that he didn't sleep much either. He said he stayed in the park and shot baskets for a long time. When it was very dark, he went home and practiced on his old drum set.

We had been **scheduling** band practice around basketball practice so Jake could be there. He was still late the next day, though.

He was out of breath when he got there. He must have run all the way.

He sat down on a chair and caught his breath. When he could breathe, he just sat there some more. He didn't take off his jacket. He didn't go over to his drums. He just sat and stared at me.

"Choices," he said. "They're tough."

That's when I knew what he was going to do. I couldn't believe it. He was going to quit the band.

"Here's the way it is," he said. "I can be *good* at both. But I can't be *great* at both. I love the band. But I love basketball more. So there it is."

Then he left. I guess he went to the park to work on becoming a great basketball player.

We sat there for a few minutes. I couldn't look at Tico and Matt. I really hated them. I didn't want to talk to them. I didn't even want to know them.

After a while, I left, too. I went up to my room and lay on my bed. I stared up at the ceiling of my room.

I didn't want to be in a band without Jake.

I didn't see Tico or Matt for two days. Then I heard them. They were out in my garage. They were playing a song Jake and I had written five years before. It sounded all right. In fact, it sounded so good that I thought Jake was back.

I ran out to the garage. Someone was playing Jake's drums. It wasn't Jake, though. It was a drummer I had never seen before.

I sat down and listened. It would take some time for this drummer to become the heartbeat of our band. He was good, though. He was very good.

After a while, I picked up my guitar and joined them. We played well together. But we needed more time to become a band. We had about one week until we opened for the

J.C. Underground. It wasn't enough time. But it would have to do.

We practiced every morning before school. We practiced after school and late at night. We practiced all weekend. By the night of the gig, we were good. We weren't perfect. But we were good.

It was the night of the show. The crowd was pouring in, and I was shaking. I couldn't do it. I needed Jake. We weren't going to get a record deal. And it would be my fault.

Somehow I walked onstage. The crowd took one look and turned away. They didn't care about us. We were too young. We were wasting their time. We weren't the band they had come to see.

Somewhere out there was a record **producer**. This was our big chance. So we started to play. The first song wasn't bad. It wasn't good either. It was my fault. I was off.

I just couldn't find the beat.

Then I saw Jake. There he was, right in front of me. He was so close that I could see the frown on his forehead. That scared me. Were we really sounding that bad?

As I hit the first note of the second song, my eyes were on Jake. I was off again. Jake knew it. I knew it, too. I couldn't get it.

Then, as the frown got worse, he began to snap his fingers. He was keeping time. I followed it. He brought me back. Suddenly, the band was together.

The crowd turned around. They stopped talking. They started to move to the music. They clapped. They cheered. They liked us. We were a band. We could do this.

I looked around at the rest of the band. They were having a great time.

I looked down at Jake. The frown was gone. He wasn't snapping his fingers. And I was playing fine.

Then, when I looked down again, he was

gone. I missed the next beat. But I found it again a few seconds later.

The crowd totally loved us.

After the gig, the record producer came backstage. He shook our hands and asked us our names. Then he said he liked us.

He said he wanted to think about it. Our chances were very good, though. So it looks like we might be getting a record deal.

We took the next day and night off. I called off practice because I wanted to spend time with Jake. I was tired.

I waited for him outside the back door of the school. He seemed glad to see me. I thanked him for being there the night before. Then I told him about the record deal. I wasn't sure how he'd take it.

"You don't mind?" I said. "It was your band. And now it looks like we'll be making it without you."

He shrugged. "It was my choice," he said. "We'll see if it was the right one."

We started walking home. "Maybe I won't make the NBA," Jake said. "Maybe I won't get a basketball **scholarship**. Maybe I'll spend my life shooting hoops in the park."

"Maybe we won't get a record deal," I said. "Maybe we'll be history in a year."

We laughed. Our lives seemed to be full of "maybes."

"I love basketball," he said. "I want to be the greatest. That takes time."

Everything takes time, I thought. And timing, I guess, is everything.

At the end of the story, Max says "timing is everything." What does he mean?

Glossary

deal *(noun)* a contract or business agreement

directions *(noun)* ways that someone or something is moving or pointing

experiment *(verb)* to try something new

gigs *(noun)* jobs for a band to play

local *(adjective)* near your house or the area where you live

producer *(noun)* a person who is in charge of a project

scheduling *(noun)* planning when events should happen *(related word: schedule)*

scholarship *(noun)* a prize that pays for you to go to college

timing *(noun)* the beat in a song *(related word: time)*